ATTACK OF THE KILLER POTATOES

Other books by the author

Spring Fever!
Spring Break
It Came From the Cafeteria

ATTACK OF THE KILLER POTATOES

PETER LERANGIS

AN
APPLE
PAPERBACK

SCHOLASTIC INC.
New York Toronto London Auckland Sydney

No part of this publication may be reproduced in whole or in part, or stored in a retrieval system, or transmitted in any form or by any means, electronic, mechanical, photocopying, recording, or otherwise, without written permission of the publisher. For information regarding permission, write to Scholastic Inc., 555 Broadway, New York, NY 10012.

ISBN 0-590-93971-8

12 11 10 9 8 7 6 5 4 3 2 1   7 8 9/9 0 1 2/0

Printed in the U.S.A.   40

First Scholastic printing, April 1997

Author's note: The events and characters portrayed herein are purely fictional. No root, tuber, or any other form of vegetable life was harmed, altered, or destroyed in the making of this book.

Attack of the Killer Potatoes

Prologue

It all started with the wart on my dad's nose, a stuffed rat, and mosquito guts.

If my dad hadn't had the wart, my mom wouldn't have noticed him. She thought he looked like a triceratops. My mom is a paleontologist, and she thinks triceratopses are way cute. So, because of that wart, my parents fell in love and were married.

If that hadn't happened, my older sister, Courtney, wouldn't have been born.

If she hadn't been born, I wouldn't have needed to scare anyone with a stuffed rat.

If it hadn't been for the rat, I wouldn't have heard about the mosquito guts.

Without those particular guts, the mess with the killer potatoes would never have happened.

And I, Arnold Mayhew, would still be an average seventh-grade kid in Middle School 27 in the city of San Dunstan.

But he had, and they did, and she was, and I did, and it happened, and I'm not.

It's that simple.

Follow?

No? Okay, I'll backtrack a bit. To a time when life was easier. To a recent sunny Friday afternoon in the basement of the San Dunstan Museum of Natural History.

It was the first day of our spring vacation.

And the last day I could even look at a potato without wanting to scream.

1

"**K**eep your eye on the bouncing bones, folks," said my best friend, Max Beekly. He picked up three huge bones from a table marked COLLIER BLUFF DINOSAUR DIG and began juggling them.

"MAX PUT THOSE DOWN YOU CAN'T DO THAT!" shrieked my big sister.

That's Courtney. She likes to talk in capital letters. It doesn't take much to upset her.

"Don't have a cow, Courtney," I said.

"If these were so important," Max said, juggling away, "they'd be on a skeleton."

I agreed. Bones are no big deal down in the basement of the San Dunstan Museum of Natural History. You trip over them. You sneeze on bone dust. If Max dropped one and it broke, no one would ever notice.

Mom works at the museum. Personally, I think she has the world's coolest job. She spends all day at dinosaur digs. You see, San Dunstan is only about an hour from the world-famous Collier Bluff bone beds. There, Mom and her colleagues have discovered seventeen new dinosaur species.

Well, maybe eighteen. Whenever she's on the verge of a new discovery, she becomes very spacey. Lately I had discovered sweatsocks in the dishwasher and a tennis racket in the freezer.

These were sure signs that something was up.

Which was why Courtney, Max, and I were waiting outside her basement office at five o'clock on the Friday before vacation. Usually we meet her after school and walk home together. Today, however, Mom was deep in conference.

And we were about to collapse from boredom.

Now Max had added another bone to his juggling act. "Have no fear, ladies and gentlemen!" he announced. "These are not your ordinary shoulder bones. They're petrified through and through!"

Unfortunately, so was Courtney.

"MAAAAX, ST-O-O-OP!" she wailed.

Down the hall, a big oak door swung open and my mom stuck her head out. "Courtney? Arnold? Would you mind keeping it down?"

Thunk! Thunk! Thunk! Thunk!

Max's bones hit the floor.

"And would you please put back the pha-langes?" Mom asked.

"The who?" Max asked.

"The toe bones!" Mom explained.

Max lifted one of those things off the floor. It was almost the size of his head. "Did you say *toe*?"

2

Mom's face grew very serious. She mumbled something to the people in the room, then walked into the hallway and shut the door behind her.

Stooping to lift one of the dropped bones, she said, "You did not see these. Understand?"

Courtney sneered at Max. "I told you they were valuable."

"*Valuable* doesn't come close to describing them," Mom said. She pulled a key out of her pocket and unlocked a door across the hall. Then she reached inside and flicked a switch.

The room was instantly bathed in harsh white light — and I nearly swallowed my tongue.

A skull jumped out at me. A skull the size of the entire room — with teeth as long and sharp as swords!

2

Courtney was on the floor. "HOOOOO-ha-ha-ha-ha!" she hooted, slapping her knees.

The skull was still there. Sitting on a low table. Grinning. As if it had planned with my obnoxious sister to scare the living daylights out of me.

"Sorry, Arnold," Mom said. "I should have warned you. It does seem to leap out, doesn't it?"

"Wh-wh-whuck —?" Max was shaking.

"I think he means to say, 'What is it?'" Courtney translated.

Mom looked left and right. When she spoke, her voice was a whisper. "We've been digging it for weeks. We had to bring it here hidden in an empty cement mixer. Kids, this discovery will set the world of paleontology on its ear. Compared to this, the tyrannosaurus is a bunny rabbit. It must be some sort of mutant. Some species with an out-of-control growth hormone." Mom grinned proudly. "We have christened it the humongosaurus. The name was my idea."

"Coooool," Max and I both said.

Courtney had this faraway look in her eye. She didn't say a thing.

Mom turned off the light and headed back into her office. "I'll be a few more minutes," she said. "We're planning security. This project must be top secret. If the news leaks out before the dig's finished, forget it. The whole site will be looted. Fossil vandals are all over the place. You can't trust anyone these days."

"Numb's the word," Max said.

"*Mum*, you dork," Courtney snapped.

Max looked shocked. "Don't call your mother names!"

Mom ignored the comments. As she pushed open her office door, she said softly over her shoulder, "And stay out of the rooms. Especially taxidermy. You remember what happened last time."

Max blushed.

"Yes, Mom," I said.

Last time meant two weeks before, when Max found the skin of a baboon face and put it on like a mask. Leaping out into the hallway, he almost gave the security guard a heart attack. Needless to say, we all got into trouble. Even Mom. Her boss threatened to fire her if she couldn't control us.

When Mom disappeared behind the door, Courtney punched her fist in the air and began dancing around. "Yyyyyyyes!"

"What are you so frisky about?" Max asked.

"I," Courtney said, "have my science fair topic!"

Max and I exchanged a look. "Uh, come again?" Max asked.

"It's perfect," Courtney replied. "A real, live bone from the biggest dinosaur in the history of the world. I'll win first place. I won't even have to do anything!"

"Earth to Courtney," Max said. "Do the words *top secret* mean anything to you?"

"I don't have to tell anyone the *name* of the dinosaur." Courtney smirked at me. "Besides, it's so much more original than your stupid topic."

"Comparing the melting points of chocolate and marshmallows in S'more-making?" I said. "I happen to think it's a great idea."

"Tell that to your teacher when she holds you back a grade," Courtney muttered as she went to the table and sorted through the bones. "Hmmm. This one's cute . . ."

Max grabbed me by the arm and pulled me away. "Don't let her talk to you like that."

"You don't think I'll flunk out, do you?" I asked.

"My motto is, don't get mad, get even."

"You said the S'mores project was a good idea, too. And we can eat the results, so it's, like, environmentally sound. I mean, I should pass, no sweat, right?"

"Who does she think she is?"

I did not like the fact that Max wasn't answering my questions.

We both tiptoed around a corner, into a long, dimly lit corridor. At the other end were a few open lab doors. We could hear bubbling noises and the soft clinking of glass.

We walked cautiously past a custodian closet. Its door was slightly ajar, but it was dark inside. Just beyond it, Max pushed open a familiar door marked TAXIDERMY, B-17.

I couldn't believe it. "Max, didn't you hear what my mom said?" I hissed.

Max rolled his eyes. "Do you think I'm going to let us be caught this time?"

"But — but —" Sputtering like a broken engine, I followed him in.

You would have, too. B-17 is the coolest room in the museum — huge and smelly, but full of stuffed animals, half-stuffed animals, and dead animal skins waiting to be stuffed.

Max went over to a huge wooden file cabinet and pulled open a drawer. "When's Courtney's birthday?" he asked.

"Not until July," I answered.

"Soon enough. Maybe we can give her an early present."

With a big grin, Max pulled a stuffed gray rat out of the drawer. A huge one. The size of a badger. Buck-toothed and goggle-eyed, too. It must have been too ugly to put on display; you could tell it had been in that drawer for ages. Its fur was all mangy and covered with dust balls.

"You are sick," I said. "Totally twisted."

"Thanks," Max replied. "Let's go!"

"If we're caught, I don't know you."

Max peered out into the corridor. He signaled me to follow. I walked on tiptoe.

The only sound was a soft beeping from a nearby lab. As Max walked, he swung the rat by its tail.

"Max!" I whispered. "Put that thing in your —"

Then, out of nowhere, a deep voice cried out, "There you are!"

We were dead meat.

3

Max dropped the rat. He and I scrambled back into the taxidermy room.

"Where did you think I was?" mumbled a gruff voice from just beyond the wall. "This is a janitor's room. I'm supposed to be the janitor."

I didn't realize I'd been holding my breath. When I exhaled, it sounded like a hurricane.

Max glared at me.

Through the wall we could hear the first voice chuckling. "How'd you manage to get the uniform?"

"The boss provides the disguises," answered the second. "I just wear them. Now cut the small talk, Dr. Nardo, and tell me what you've got for us."

I mouthed the words "Let's get out of here" to Max.

"No way," he mouthed back, pressing his ear to the wall.

I did not like the sound of this at all.

The first voice, Dr. Nardo's, dropped to a whisper. "This is a big one, Ralphie. Big science. Big bucks."

"That's what you said about the caveman tooth," said the man named Ralphie. "Turned out to be a monkey's. The boss needs something he can sell, pal. If you can't make him a cool billion, you're in trouble."

"Ralphie, this is better than a billion," said Dr. Nardo. "What would you say if I told you we'd discovered a Humongosaurus, the biggest dinosaur ever?"

That was Mom's secret! Boy, was I boiling. I wanted to confront these guys, but Max shot me a warning glance.

"*Another lizard?*" Ralphie said. "Aw, man, that's boring —"

"And what if I told you that nearby it, I found an ancient mosquito embedded in amber?" Dr. Nardo went on. "And that the mosquito's stomach contains perfectly preserved humongosaurus DNA?"

"Dan? Who's that?"

"Not D-A-N. *DNA!* The stuff that contains the dinosaur's genes!"

"You think I'm stupid? Dinosaurs didn't wear jeans!"

"*Genes*, Ralphie! Chemicals that contain instructions for building a creature's body. If you know the code of a creature's DNA, you can create a clone — from scratch!"

"Hey, I saw a movie about this. Are you telling me you can make a whole dinosaur?"

"Not exactly. The DNA I found is just a fragment — but a great one. We've made a protein with it. I believe it may be . . . the humongosaurus growth hormone." Dr. Nardo said that slowly, as if it were the most important discovery in the world.

"Okay, cool," Ralphie said. "So what's the big whoop?"

"Just imagine, Ralphie. Inside every living thing — plant, animal, and human — is a growth hormone. It's like a timer. When we reach a certain size, it says, 'Ehhhhh . . . time's up! Stop growing!' For me, it happened when I was five feet nine. For my tomato plants, when they're a couple of feet high. But for the humongosaurus, it didn't kick in until it was the size of a ten-story building."

Ralphie whistled softly. "I get it. If you transplant this thing to a mouse, say —"

"It would nibble your house down in four gulps."

Ralphie cackled with glee. "Farmers can use it to grow bigger crops, bigger cattle."

"Basketball team owners can grow players tall enough to dunk sitting down."

"And if we own the hormone, they all have to pay us! Big bucks! *Humongous* bucks!"

"Which is why no one at the museum must find out," Dr. Nardo said. "They'll want to share the DNA with the entire scientific community! They'll actually want to benefit humankind."

"The nerve of those jerks!"

"So, just give me a few months to analyze —"

"*A few months?*"

"We have to be sure the protein is growth hormone. It may not be. It has a similar structure to nasal fluid."

"Whaaaat? Listen, Nardo. The boss isn't interested in dinosaur snot. If it's growth hormone, we'll sell it on the black market, and you're rich. If not, the deal's off. Give it to me and our lab'll test it. Now, where is it?"

Max and I looked at each other. His face was pale.

I could see the headlines now: SCIENTIST AND CROOK NABBED FOR MAJOR THEFT: MIDDLE SCHOOL KIDS KNEW ALL ABOUT IT, JAILED FOR CONSPIRACY.

Dr. Nardo sighed. "You'll find it in my section of lab B-29. I can't remove it now, or my colleagues will be suspicious. You'll have to come back later, after they've all gone home. When you're cleaning up, look behind the Bunsen burner. You'll see a flask with fizzy liquid and a beakerful of bubbles. Near the beaker is a rack of test tubes. The tubes are labeled with geometric shapes. Take the one labeled with a Rubik's Cube. That contains the substance in a special potion. Now, be careful. It's precious stuff."

"Wait. Where's this precious potion? In the flask or the beaker?"

"You'll find the precious potion in the tube with the cube —"

"Behind the Bunsen burner near the beaker with the bubbles?"

"It's perfectly apparent in the back on the rack!"

"The beaker with the bubbles?"

"No, the tube with the cube!" Dr. Nardo said. "Got it?"

"I think so."

"Repeat it back to me."

Ralphie exhaled loudly. "I'll find the Bunsen bubbles near the potion with the burner on the rack with the cube near the beaker on my sneaker —"

"Listen! It's absolutely simple. Behind the Bunsen burner, on the rack in the back, is the tube with the cube, which contains the precious potion!"

"Near the flask with the fizzes?"

"No, the beaker with the bubbles. The fluid in the flask is a can of Coca Cola that I split with my assistant."

"So the flask with the fizzes has the can of Coca Cola, but the rack in the back's near the beaker with the bubbles."

"And the rack in the back has the tube with the cube."

"Which contains the precious potion?"

"It's perfectly apparent. Now, can you remember all that?"

"Uh . . . sure."

"Good."

"Let's go. It stinks in here."

The two men began bustling around the closet. Max and I shrank deeper into the taxidermy room and jumped under a rhinoceros hide.

"AGGGGGHHHHHHHHHH!"

The scream made us both jump. I peered out from under the hide. The stuffed rat was in the hallway where Max had dropped it, facing the janitor's closet. We could hear two sets of heavy footsteps running away to the left.

As Max and I untangled ourselves from the hide, Courtney appeared in the right side of the doorway. "What are you two screaming about? The hippo is sitting on you?"

"It's a rhino," I said. "And it wasn't us screaming."

Courtney kicked the stuffed rat back into the room. "Don't leave your dinner on the floor."

With that, she stomped away.

I began pacing. "We have to call the police."

Max looked at me as if I were nuts. "Are you nuts?"

"It's wrong for them to steal, Max. Scientists should share —"

"Exactly right! Which is why we are going to take it before they do."

I burst out laughing. "Something must be wrong with my hearing. I actually thought you said *we* were going to take the growth hormone!"

"Hey, you were the one worried about your science fair project, right? This would be perfect! It'll make Courtney's look like baby stuff!"

"*You're* nuts."

"Step right up, ladies and gentlemen, see what happens when Arnold Mayhew feeds humongosaurus hormone to a hamster!"

"Max, we can't do it, it's wrong," I said. "Besides, what if it isn't what he thinks it is? What if it's dinosaur mucus?"

"Call it Jurassic boogers. It'll still be more interesting than a stupid bone."

"No, Max. No way."

Max sighed. "All right, have it your way. Courtney can help me. She'd love this for her project. *Oh, Co-o-o-o-urtn —*"

"Stop!" I said.

Now, let me say this right now: I did not want to steal that stuff. But what were the alternatives? (A) Let the two crooks take it later, (b) let my sister use it for her science fair project, and (c) do what Max suggested.

(A) was out. As for (b), well, I did not want my sister to win a science fair prize because of my hard work. Besides, if she were caught, she might be hauled away in handcuffs. Which, come to think of it, didn't sound too bad.

But if I chose (c), I could turn the test tube in to my mom, who could return it to the museum and maybe get a cash reward.

How wrong could that be? Mom doesn't make much money at her job. Neither does my dad, who works for a canned meatloaf company. Every year I ask them if we can go to Hollywood for vacation and every year they laugh and say they're putting aside all their extra money for Courtney's college education.

With a nice cash reward, they wouldn't have that excuse anymore.

So what's a little theft, if it's for a good cause?

"Okay," I said, "I'll do it."

4

I peeked around the corner of the corridor. Courtney was still examining bones. Mom's office door was still closed. No janitors or scientists in sight.

"Coast is clear," I whispered.

Max turned and walked past the taxidermy room. He was whistling at the top of his lungs.

"What are you doing that for?" I asked.

"So no one will be suspicious," he said. "When we get to lab B-29, we pretend we belong here."

"*Two twelve-year-olds?*"

A balding guy with a white lab coat and thick glasses stuck his head out the open door of lab B-29. "Will you kids keep it down?"

Max shot him a suspicious look. "Are you Nardo?"

The guy looked flustered. "No, not Nardo. Naughton. Nardo's gone for the day. Are you his —?"

"Sons!" said Max.

"Nephews!" I said at the same time.

"Both!" Max blurted out. "Our mom was married to his brother. Then he died and she married Uncle Nardo — I mean, Uncle Doctor. I mean —"

"Wait a minute!" Dr. Naughton narrowed his eyes at us. "Then how could you have mistaken *me* for *him*?"

"Uh . . . we haven't seen him since we were orphaned!" Max blurted out. "But he sent a note saying we could visit him at home if we brought him his Coca Cola from the lab."

Dr. Naughton looked over his shoulder toward a large, cluttered lab table in the back of the room. Among racks and beakers and flasks was a sheet of yellow legal paper. I could make out the words DO NOT EVEN *THINK* OF DISTURBING! — DR. NARDO.

"In the beaker with the bubbles or the flask with the fizzes?" asked Dr. Naughton.

I blurted, "The beaker."

Max blurted, "The flask."

"Make up your minds, and make it quick." Dr. Naughton waved us toward the table and went back to his work.

Huddled over their own experiments, a couple of other scientists eyed us warily. Max tried to whistle, and I joined him. But we were both so nervous we could only blow.

Fffff . . . fffff . . . ffff.

"Great," I muttered. "We sound like two whales. Mr. and Mrs. Moby Dick on shore leave."

Max glared at me. "Am I the wife or you?"

"Never mind!"

When we reached the table, I couldn't help gasping. Crammed onto it were about a dozen electronic instruments, each with moving dials, each wired to a massive computer. Different-colored fluids burbled and fizzed in strangely shaped containers.

I looked at Dr. Nardo's warning. My body clenched up. Who knew what kinds of weird stuff he had on this thing, what kinds of secret poisons and hormones and potions?

What were we getting ourselves into?

"M-M-Max, let's just get out of here —"

"Let's see . . . the tube with the bubbles has the potion with the fizzes . . ."

"Max —"

"Or was it the blubber with the cubby has the flipper with the flubber . . ."

"We could be arrested —"

"I remember!" Max said. "The fleaker with the bizzies has the potion from the ocean, but the can of Coca Cola's in the tube with the cube!"

At the other end of the room, Dr. Naughton was whispering with some of his colleagues. They were glaring at us suspiciously.

"Max, they *know*!" I whispered. "Let's get out of here!"

Now Max came around the table. I grabbed his arm and yanked him toward the door.

CRRRRASHHHH! went the equipment on Dr. Nardo's lab table.

"Call security!" shouted Dr. Naughton.

Two of the other scientists scrambled for the phone.

I bolted for the door. *"Come on, Max!"*

20

5

"**H**ey! Where are you two going?"

Max and I froze at the sound of the deep voice. We were in the corridor, heading for the turn-off to Mom's office.

Max spun around, his hands in the air. "Don't shoot! I have a wife and two small children!"

Two beefy guys in museum security uniforms walked toward us. "Very funny, short stuff."

Dr. Naughton was standing outside lab B-29, arms crossed. "Those kids messed up Dr. Nardo's lab!" he called out.

Max glowered at him. "And we thought you were our friend!"

The guards grabbed our arms. "You two here alone?"

"M-M-My mom works around the corner!" I stammered.

Breaking and entering. I could hear the judge's pronouncement now. I pictured bars. Big, iron prison bars. I saw myself sitting on a cement bench with a long gray beard, marking off the days on a wall.

"Leggo, ya big lugs!" Max said, squirming. "You haven't read us our rights! I demand a lawyer!"

Leg irons. Dirty striped uniforms.

We stumbled around the corner. Courtney was still standing by the bone table. She was staring at us, dumbfounded.

"Courtney, these guys are going to dump us in the lake with cement shoes!" Max called out. "Stop them!"

Guard towers. Razor wires. Attack dogs.

The guard let go of my arm. "You know these guys?"

"The dumb one is my brother," Courtney said with a sneer. "The ugly one is a stray."

Mom poked her head out of the conference room door. "What's going on?"

"These two have been making mischief in the labs, ma'am," said one of the guards.

"Arnold Mayhew, must I ground you tomorrow?" Mom asked sternly.

Ground me? Yikes! Max and I were supposed to go to a baseball game, the season opener. "No! Please please please please!"

The guards gave each other a weary look. "You stay out of the labs, okay, fellas?" the second one said. "Ask your mom to buy you a chemistry set."

As the guards ambled away, Mom gave me a

we'll-discuss-this-later look and ducked back into the room.

"That knucklehead sprained my arm," Max murmured. "I'll sue!"

I whirled around to face him. "Max, I will never, ever listen to you again. It's a good thing we didn't take anything. We could have been arrested. We could have ended up in the slammer —"

"Arrested?" Courtney asked. "For what?"

I plopped myself down on the floor, arms folded. "Conspiracy with an ugly fourteen-year-old girl to steal a humongosaurus bone."

Well, Courtney chickened out of stealing the bone. Max was strangely silent to me while we waited for Mom. After she finally emerged, we all rode the subway downtown from the museum station to 96th Street, where we live.

It was rush hour, so we had to stand, all scrunched together. Courtney was to my right, trying desperately not to touch me. Every time I was jostled close to her, she'd hold up her palms, on which she'd scribbled "CP" for Cootie Protection. (Mature, huh?) Mom was to Courtney's right, attempting to read a newspaper.

When Max kicked me in the ankle, I turned to bop him on the head.

But the strange grin on his face stopped me. He had pulled open his jacket slightly so I could see inside. Peeking out of his inner pocket was a large test tube.

A tube labeled with a Rubik's Cube.

"Max, you fool!" I said through gritted teeth.

"We *wanted* to take this!" Max reminded me. "Remember?"

"That was before we were caught! Now they know us. When Dr. Nardo notices what's gone, he'll track us down!"

"Nahh. Not unless he's dying of thirst for warm, flat Coca Cola."

I looked as closely as I could at the tube. The liquid inside was dark brown. "How do you know for sure?"

"Remember? 'The can of Coca Cola's in the tube with the cube'!"

"That was the beaker with the bubbles!"

"No. 'You'll find the precious potion in the flask with the fizzes near the rack in the back' — which I was trying to grab before I was so rudely pulled away —"

Courtney's arm lunged across me and snatched the test tube from Max. "What are you *hiding*, guys?" she asked.

Max and I both tried to grab the tube, but Courtney was too fast. "Some secret formula?" she taunted, holding it in the air.

Mom was looking up. My heart was dropping to my toes.

"It's Coke!" Max insisted.

Mom chuckled. "Must be Pete Nardo's. He loves to put his soft drinks in his lab containers."

Courtney pulled the cork stopper off the tube. "Mmm," she said, "I'm thirsty."

She lifted her arm and cocked her head back to take a swig.

6

"**N**O-O-O-O-O-O!"

I blocked Courtney's arm.

"Oh, great, Arnold, bruise me," Courtney whined. "Now I'll have to wear long-sleeve shirts until June!"

I grabbed the test tube and the cork. Quickly I stoppered the tube and put it in my pocket. "If you drink that, you might be wearing circus tents," I grumbled. "Humongodork, biggest awkward teenager in history."

"You don't mean . . ." The color drained from Courtney's face. "It wasn't *diet* Coke?"

"Maybe something much worse," I said.

"Yeah," Max piped up. "Mesozoic mucus."

The train lurched to a sudden halt. Mom folded her paper and said, "This is our stop!"

I crossed my eyes at Courtney. She stuck her tongue at me and headed out the door.

"Why'd you stop her?" Max said as we elbowed our way onto the station platform. "She would have gotten a mouthful of Coke mixed with Dr. Nardo's spit."

"Either that or we'd have to cut a hole up to your apartment just to fit her."

"Ha ha."

In case you haven't guessed, Max lives in the apartment directly above ours. Even better, Max's bedroom is over Courtney's. When she's being especially rotten, I just tell Max to drop a bowling ball on his floor every few minutes. The results are very amusing.

By the time Max and I reached the sidewalk, Mom and Courtney were already picking through the fruits and vegetables at the corner market.

I clutched the test tube tightly. "I say we return this now, tell Mom we forgot something at the museum —"

"Relax, Arnold. We can just dump it down the sink."

"Oh, right. Sure. Next thing you know we'll be attacked by sewer rats the size of Land Rovers."

Courtney was suddenly right behind us, eavesdropping. "What are you guys talking about?" she said with a sly grin.

"The pimple at the end of your nose," Max replied.

"You think I'm stupid enough to fall for that trick?" Courtney asked. "It's about the stuff in the bottle, right? You stole it, didn't you? And it's not really Coca Cola."

"Okay, I admit," Max said with a sigh. "It's Pepsi."

"Kids, have you seen the bok choy?" Mom called out.

"I think so," I answered, scanning the sidewalk. "Here, bok choy! Here, boy!"

"It's a vegetable, you doof," Courtney said. "Now, let me see —"

She reached for my test tube. But this time I was too fast for her. I pulled it back quickly.

"I'll ask Mr. Han about the bok choy," Mom called out, walking into the store. "You kids behave."

"You slimy, stinking little —" Courtney lunged toward me, practically knocking over a stack of oranges.

I stumbled backward. As I flailed my arms, Courtney took the test tube and turned away.

Max sprinted around and snatched it out of her hand. Courtney tore after him.

"Over here!" I called, running like a wide receiver.

Max tossed the test tube. Courtney blocked it with her fingertips. It sailed into the air, wobbling.

Max, Courtney, and I all dived for it at once.

The tube brushed against my fingers. It landed on a pile of white Idaho potatoes. With a sharp tinkle, it broke into a thousand pieces.

The brown liquid began oozing downward.

"Mom! Come see what Arnold did!" Courtney shrieked, running into the store.

Max and I were rooted to the spot. Staring.

Wherever the liquid came into contact with the potatoes, they were glowing. Pulsating. First a pinkish tinge, then green.

"What the —?" Max gasped.

In a moment the green faded, and the potatoes were back to their normal color. As if nothing had happened.

I glanced around. None of the other shoppers seemed to have noticed.

"I have news for you, Max," I said. "That stuff was not Coca Cola."

Max nodded solemnly. "Or dinosaur boogers."

I had a feeling we were in trouble.

Big trouble.

7

I quickly took off my backpack. "Load up."

"Whaaaaat?" Max exclaimed.

"What other choice do we have? We have to get rid of these." I began dumping potatoes into my pack.

"Where are we going to put them?"

"I don't know! We'll decide that later! Hurry!"

As Max started loading potatoes into his pack, Courtney ran out the door. She was pulling Mom by the hand. "Look what they did!"

I shoved the last few spuds into my pack and zipped up. The potato stand was now empty.

"Hi, Mom!" I said.

Mom was staring at my pack, which now looked as if it contained a small moose. "What on earth —?"

"Potatoes," I said as cheerily as I could.

"But you hate potatoes," Mom said.

"Besides," Courtney added, "they're covered with —"

"As I always say to Arnold, you can never have too many spuds," Max cut in. "High taste, premium carbohydrates, attractive price! I think he's beginning to agree."

"Yes, imagine the possibilities," I spoke up. "Roast potatoes, potato salad, baked potatoes —"

"Potato pancakes," Max butted in, "potato soup, potato bread, potato sundaes —"

"*Potato sundaes?*" Courtney said. "Don't listen, Mom. They want to buy the potatoes because they spilled this stuff they took from the —"

"I'm too tired to argue," Mom said, turning toward the cash register. "Bring the packs here, boys. Arnold, you can pay me back out of your allowance."

"Ha!" Courtney crowed triumphantly.

Max and I dragged our backpacks toward the cashier. "I'll bill you," I snarled.

Dragging those packs home was like pulling water buffaloes across a swamp. If our apartment building hadn't had an elevator, I think I would have dropped dead with exhaustion.

My dad greeted us at the door. Our little Lhasa Apso, Yappy, went wild when he saw our packs. He jumped all over them, barking and panting like crazy.

Dad burst out laughing. "He sure seems happy. What's in the packs? You each brought home a fire hydrant?"

"Potatoes," Mom explained. "Arnold has a craving."

Max and I led the way into the apartment. We dropped our packs inside the kitchen door. I could smell Dad's famous orange-flavored porkchops cooking in the oven.

"Don't unload these potatoes," I said. "Max and I will take care of them in a minute."

As Courtney and Mom bustled into the kitchen with bags of groceries, Dad puttered around preparing dinner.

Yap! Yap-yap-yap-yap-yap! yapped Yappy.

I pushed Max into my bedroom and closed the door. "Now what?" I asked.

Max shrugged. "Invite me to dinner. I personally love mashed potatoes. Maybe some of them are usable."

"*How do you want us to find out, Max?* Take a bite and see if we grow?"

"All right, all right, let's burn them in the park."

"The rangers will be on us in a second."

"Dump them in the reservoir?"

"Oh, terrific idea. So the whole city can share it!"

"Wait. Isn't the growth hormone already, like, absorbed? I mean, if it's part of the potato, does it sort of graft onto the potatoes' molecules or something, so it can't harm us? Or does anyone who eats the potato also become affected —"

"*How should I know?*"

"Maybe we should call Dr. Nardo —"

My dad's voice wafted in through the closed door. "Where are we going to *put* all these?"

Zoom. Out we went.

Dad was busy taking potatoes out of my pack and shoving them into the fridge.

"Didn't you hear me —?" I began.

"Put them back!" Max blurted out. "We have to return them."

I elbowed Dad aside and began pulling potatoes out of the fridge. "They overcharged us. Max saw Mr. Han leaning on the scale."

"But Mr. Han would never do that —"

Plop. In went the last spud. I quickly zipped up the pack. "We'll be right back!"

I caught a glimpse of Mom, Dad, and Courtney as we left. If you put speech bubbles overhead, they'd say "Duh," "Huh?" and "Wha —?"

Out the door and down the elevator we went.

I pressed B for Basement. "We'll get shovels and bury these things in the park."

"What if they grow?" Max asked.

"In that soil?" I said. "Dogs use it all day."

Max almost gagged. "I hope they're *long* shovels."

They were. We snatched two of them, rode the elevator to the lobby floor, and lugged everything outside.

One of the best things about our apartment building is that it's right around the corner from Olmstead Park, the biggest park in the whole city.

Just inside the 96th Street entrance is a field. Well, it was a field once, before the local dogs turned it into a big dirt patch.

We pulled the packs past the subway entrance and into the park. It was getting dark, and we set the packs down in a shadowy area just outside the pool of streetlamp light.

"Start digging," I said.

"It's nighttime!" Max replied. "How can we see what we're stepping in?"

"Don't worry about that now!"

We began shoveling. The soil was hard as a rock, but we managed to make a hole about two feet deep and six feet across.

Quickly we threw the potatoes in it, tossed the soil over them, and began stomping it flat.

"Done," Max said. "Problem solved. Life goes on. Now, can I come over for dinner or what?"

"Sure, Max, sure," I said.

As we walked out of the park, I glanced over my shoulder.

I stopped dead in my tracks. The ground was glowing green.

"Max, come here!" I rubbed my eyes.

Max ran to my side. "What?"

"The ground!"

Max squinted into the park.

The glowing had stopped. The ground was normal again.

"The ground what?" Max asked.

"It was glowing," I said.

Max shook his head. "Let's go home, Arnold. You need some rest."

8

Thunk. The elevator door closed behind us on the fifth floor as we headed toward Max's apartment.

"Maybe you were seeing things," Max said. "You're under a lot of stress."

"*You* saw the potatoes glowing at the grocery store. This was just like that."

Max rang his doorbell. "What do you think it means?"

"Maybe the hormone is seeping into the ground."

"Can dirt grow?"

"Dirt isn't a living thing!"

"So what's the problem? So the hormone has a glowy, throbby, greenish effect. Big deal."

Max's mom opened the door. Behind her, I could see Mr. Beekly eating dinner with Max's brother. "You were perhaps waiting for a private invitation?" Mrs. Beekly asked.

"Sorry, Mom," Max said. "Arnold and I were

wrapped up in a genetics project. Can I have dinner at Arnold's?"

I thought Mrs. Beekly's eyes would pop right out. "You have the nerve to ask me —"

CRRRRAASSHHHH!

The noise was from downstairs. From my apartment.

"Got to go!" I shouted.

"Me too!" Max added.

I turned and ran down the stairs with Max at my heels.

Halfway to the fourth floor I could hear my dad yelling, "Back! Back!"

I fished my keys out of my pocket and opened the door. "What hap —?"

Courtney was backing into the front hallway, her hands clutching the sides of her face. "L-L-L-Look!"

My eyes darted toward the kitchen. Mom and Dad were putting buckets on the tile floor.

Steaming white goop was flowing over the top of the stove. It dribbled down the front in thick chunks, landing in the buckets with a dull plop.

"What's this stuff?" I asked, running into the kitchen.

Dad was cracking up. "Mashed potatoes! I — I guess I must have used too much milk!"

"Looks like you used *yeast*!" Mom said.

I did not believe my eyes. My heart leaped up to my throat so fast I almost choked.

"*Mashed potatoes? Where did you get the potatoes?*" I yelled.

"From the ones you brought home," Dad replied. "They looked fresh. I figured, hey, why not? So I took a few, cooked them up, and —"

"*Didn't you hear me say not to touch them?*"

"Arnold Mayhew, don't talk to your father in that tone of voice!" Mom scolded.

Swallowing hard, I lifted one of the buckets. It weighed a ton. The stuffy-sweet smell of mashed potatoes wafted up from it. "How many did you use?" I asked.

Dad shrugged. "Four . . . five. I don't know."

"Oh, no," I murmured to myself. "Oh, no, don't tell me . . ."

"*Four or five?*" Max exclaimed.

His eyes were buggy. And his face was as white as the bubbling mass in the bucket.

9

*C*CHHHHHHRRRRRRRRR . . .

The sink disposal ground away at the last of the mashed potatoes. Well, almost the last. A potful was still on the stove. I had my eye on it.

My hands were shaking as I stood over the sink.

We had stolen the hormone. No doubt about it. It was in the tube with the cube.

And it had nearly taken over my kitchen.

I was dying to talk to Max about it, but I couldn't. Not with my unsuspecting family around.

All we could do was give each other looks. Looks that said, *If this is what four or five potatoes will do . . .*

What was going to happen to the ones we buried? I kept sneaking glances out the kitchen window, toward the park.

Dad was mopping the floor. Courtney had locked herself in the bathroom in fear and was refusing to come out. Mom and Max were taking food to the table for dinner.

The porkchops smelled fantastic and the salad looked great. Frankly, though, my appetite was out the window.

"Well," Dad said as he finished up, "look on the bright side. We had to throw out all those delicious spuds, but there are still plenty left to eat!"

He took the pot off the stove and headed for the dining room.

I ran after him. "No! Dad, we can't eat that stuff!"

With a sickening *thwap*, he ladled a lump of mashed potatoes onto each plate. "Sure we can. This part didn't fall on the floor."

Max grabbed my shoulder and whispered into my ear, "Is it edible?"

"*I don't know!*" I replied.

"Come 'n' ge-e-e-et it!" Dad shouted.

Courtney slumped in from the bathroom. She was eyeing the dining room table as if it were a sleeping crocodile. "Is it . . . safe?"

Mom shrugged. "Your dad seems to think so."

We gathered around the table and sat. The chops were still steaming. The mashed potatoes? They were smothered with peas, carrots, and gravy.

"Okay, time for grace!" Dad announced cheerily.

We all bowed our heads and closed our eyes.

"Well, I'd like to begin," Dad said in a low, serious voice, "by mentioning all our great hopes for Mom's success. Each day she comes closer and closer to assembling the humongosaurus skeleton. And someday, we'll be sitting here with a Nobel Prize staring at us from the mantel —"

"Oh, Eugene, stop!" Mom said with a giggle.

That was when I felt the first drip. A warm, thick glop on my right thigh.

My eyes sprang open.

"EEEEWWWWWWW!" Courtney screamed, leaping up.

I pushed my chair back. The mashed potatoes had spilled over my plate, landing in my lap.

I glanced around the table. The potatoes were cascading off every plate.

"*Yap! Yap-yap-yap-yap-yap!*" Yappy was in heaven, running around and lapping the stuff up.

"Elspeth, what is happening?" Dad asked.

"I — I —" Before my mom could speak a second word, Max and I cleared the plates and ran them into the kitchen. I grabbed a fork and began to scrape the potatoes into the sink.

Now the little metal catch-all in the drain was bouncing around. Below it was a low, gurgling sound.

I felt a soft thud against my shin. The sink cupboard was opening slowly. To my right, the dishwasher door was pushing out.

"Oh no . . ." Max muttered.

"What's going on here?" Dad exclaimed.

"AAAAAAGHHHHH!" shrieked Courtney.

Cans and bottles fell from the cupboard, crashing to the floor. From the dishwasher, dirty bowls and plates spilled out.

Behind them both came thick, puffy lumps of mashed potatoes!

10

"*IT'S ATTACKING US!*" Courtney's voice was so loud I think I lost partial hearing in my left ear.

The stuff was billowing onto the floor, rising up like a warm snowdrift.

"Bucket brigade!" Dad commanded.

Mom was already pulling buckets from the closet. She, Max, Dad, and I began scooping.

Courtney did the heavy-duty screaming in the kitchen doorway. "*Why is it doing that?*"

"Don't panic," Mom said with a panicked voice. "There's probably a simple explanation. A hydration problem of some sort. Possibly brought on by a highly active photosensitive, hydrophilic bacterium of unusually accelerated growth properties."

"Uh, yeah, just what I thought," Dad said, madly dumping potatoes into a bucket. "But what do we do with this stuff?"

"Open a restaurant?" Max suggested.

"Where does the apartment trash go?" I asked.

"Some of it is recycled," Mom replied, "and some is burned in the basement incinerator —"

"That's it!" I shouted.

Max was heading for the door with two buckets. "Burn, baby, burn!"

Well, it took us seven trips with five buckets, but we did it. Every last ounce of mashed potatoes was tossed into the incinerator. It was all smoke and ashes now.

Afterward I walked Max back upstairs to his apartment. I was in a blind panic. "It's going to drop from the sky, Max. Like acid rain. I just know it."

"That makes no sense, Arnold," Max replied. "This is a growth hormone, not a radioactive substance."

"*Makes no sense?* My dad just cooked up four potatoes that turned into Mount Saint Helens, and you're telling me I make no sense?"

"Arnold, I'm upset, too, but we have to keep cool —"

"How can I keep cool? What about the potatoes we buried? What's going to happen to them?"

"Relax. They weren't cooked. I think it's the cooking that activated the hormone. Something about the high temperature. It's elementary science."

"I hope you're right."

Max's door opened. His mom and dad were standing there, looking like executioners at the gallows.

Max gulped. "You think you have problems?" he said out of the side of his mouth.

Max trudged inside and the door slammed behind him. I could hear muffled shouting as I went back to my apartment.

That night I tumbled into bed, totally exhausted. But I couldn't fall asleep. Mom was on the Internet in her bedroom, trying to download information on fast-growing mashed potatoes. Dad was pacing the floor, talking to himself about the use of the potatoes in canned meatloaf. Courtney was locked in her room, snoring.

Every couple of minutes, I kept looking out my window. My room has a great view of the park. At this time of year, when the trees are just beginning to grow leaves, I can see the patch of dirt inside the stone wall.

It was black. Pitch black. Cars and taxis whizzed by as always, and an old man lazily walked his dog.

No glow, no spuds. Nothing.

As the night grew older, I relaxed a little.

Maybe Max had been right. Maybe the hormone did have to be exposed to high temperature. Who knew? On a raw, early-April night in San Dunstan, the stuff might even freeze.

I drifted into sleep sometime after two A.M. I twisted and turned the whole night.

Whomp! Whomp! Whomp!

The booming noises from upstairs woke me up. I flicked on my bedroom light and looked at my clock: 6:31.

Whomp! Whomp! Whomp!

That was Max's signal. It meant I had to call him right away.

I ran out of my room, groping along the darkened hallway for the light switch. When I made it to the kitchen phone, I tapped out Max's number.

"Arnold, wake up!" his voice greeted me. "You have to come up here!"

I was upstairs in under a minute. Max was standing in his open front doorway.

He cracked up when he saw my pajamas. "Little Mermaid?"

Oops. I had forgotten what I was wearing. "Hand-me-downs from Courtney," I muttered.

"Follow me."

He disappeared inside. I ran after him, into his bedroom. He shut the door and flicked on an overhead light.

It was pretty chilly, but I knew that Max liked to sleep with windows open, even in the winter.

But the room looked different. Plants were growing into his room through the open window. Long-stemmed plants with green and reddish-purple leaves.

"Don't tell me," I said. "You woke me up at six-thirty in the morning to show me a plant collection?"

"They're not plants," Max said. "They're vines, Arnold. Potato vines! They're growing about an inch a minute."

"Oh, no!" I could feel the blood rushing from my face. "They're coming all the way from the park?"

Max shook his head. "No, Arnold. From downstairs. From your sister's bedroom!"

11

COURTNEY'S ROOM
ALL OTHERS 4BIDDEN!!!!
ARNOLD, IF U EVEN TRY,
I WILL TELL DEENA BLODGETT
2 SMOTHER U WITH
WET KISSES
WHENEVA SHE SEES U!!!!

I hate Deena Blodgett. She has big slobbery lips. And she does do absolutely anything Courtney tells her to do.

Believe me, Courtney's warning has kept me out of her room for months.

But this morning was an exception.

I gripped Courtney's rattly doorknob and turned slowly.

"Hurry up!" Max urged from behind me.

"Sssssh." Gently I pushed.

The rhythmic sound of Courtney's snoring grew louder. The door opened a crack and I could see her posters on the wall to the right. I pushed a little more and noticed the door seemed awfully heavy . . . .

Thud! Something hard bopped me on top of the head. Brown liquid was suddenly oozing down past my ears.

"Yeow!" I touched the wet mess around my ears, then smelled my fingers. It nearly knocked me out. "What is this stuff?"

Max was cracking up. "Nice hair, Arnold."

Courtney got out of bed and picked a plastic cup off the floor. "It's prune juice. I set it on top of the door every night. This batch is about a week old."

"*Prune juice?*" I exclaimed. "*What normal girl booby-traps her bedroom door with prune juice every night?*"

"What normal boy tries to break into his sister's room at five in the morning?" Courtney asked.

"Six thirty-seven," Max said.

"Did either of you geniuses read the sign?" Courtney asked.

But I wasn't listening. My eyes were riveted on Courtney's windowsill.

A potato was sitting in a pool of water among shards of broken glass. A potato the size of a football. A potato whose hairy roots extended to the floor like a long, strange beard. A potato that had sprouted vines, which wound upward through the opening in Courtney's window.

"Courtney, where did you get that?" I asked.

Courtney turned toward the window and gasped. "Oh, no. Mom's going to kill me! That was her nicest vase."

"Not the vase," I snapped. "The potato! Did you take it from my backpack yesterday?"

Courtney shrugged uncomfortably. "Well, I need *something* for my science fair project if I can't use the humongosaurus bone —"

"Let's get it!" Max stormed toward the room, but stopped short at the doorway. "There's no more prune juice, is there?"

I ducked into the kitchen and brought back a knife.

Courtney blanched. "*HELP! MY BROTHER IS A HOMICIDAL MANIAC!*"

I ran past her, toward the potato.

"*STAY AWAY FROM MY SCIENCE FAIR PROJECT!*" Courtney roared.

"Kids!" came Dad's groggy voice from inside my parents' bedroom. "Can't you think of anything quiet to do?"

Snnnip! I cut away the vine that was growing out the window.

Courtney grabbed my arm and twisted it.

"Yeeeeeeow!" I screamed as the scissors dropped to the floor.

"Out," Courtney said in a low, threatening voice. "Just get out!"

"Can't you see?" I asked. "The potato isn't normal, Courtney."

"It's a supernatural spud," Max chimed in. "A mutant tuber —"

"Look, you were right about the stuff Max and I stole," I cut in. "It wasn't Coke. It was a growth hormone, okay?"

"So that's what happened to the mashed potatoes . . ." Courtney said, a smile creeping slowly across her face.

"You know what can happen when you fool with Mother Nature," Max said. "You've seen *The Fish That Saved Pittsburgh.*"

"*The Blob,*" I added.

Max stuck out his hand, palm up. "So just give us the potato so we can destroy it and not disturb the balance of life on earth."

"This is soooo fantastic!" Courtney was pacing back and forth excitedly, as if we weren't there. "I'll win a prize, I know it. A prize? I'll get national attention. I'll be on *The Tonight Show* —"

"She's bonkers," Max whispered.

I edged closer to the window. When Courtney turned away, I reached for the potato.

Her hand darted out and grabbed my arm. "Touch that, Arnold Mayhew, and Deena Blodgett will be grafted to your side for life."

I gulped. When my sister has that look, I know she means business. I needed another strategy.

"Come on, Max," I said meekly, heading out her door.

"But — but —" Max sputtered.

"Courtney's right. This could land her on the front page of the San Dunstan *Sun-Times*. We shouldn't stand in her way."

"But you — but I —"

When Courtney slammed her door shut, I sprinted to my room. "Wait here while I change."

"Arnold, I'm ashamed of you," Max hissed. "How can you give up so easily?"

"Who said anything about giving up?"

In minutes I was in sweats and sneakers. I burst out of my room, then sprinted to the coat closet and grabbed a jacket. "We're going back to your room."

We took the stairs two at a time. Max had re-membered his keys, which was great, because his whole family was still asleep.

We tiptoed to his room and shut the door. The vine I'd snipped was already beginning to shrivel and droop. I went to the window and looked down. Outside Max's room, the metal fire escape led straight to an alley, with a landing on each floor.

I looked at my watch. "Right about now," I said, "Courtney is starting her forty-five-minute shower. My parents are getting up and making coffee. No one is in Courtney's room."

Max gazed out onto the fire escape. His face instantly lost color. "You don't mean . . .?"

I pulled open his window all the way. The landing of the fire escape was rusty and chipped, and a few metal slats were missing.

"It's safe, isn't it?" I asked.

"*Safe?*" Max's voice was a squeak. "I — I don't know. I've never been out there. I'm afraid of heights."

"But you've lived on the fifth floor your whole life!"

"I live on *this* side of the window, Arnold! I happen to like it that way!"

"Now look who wants to give up," I mumbled, hoisting myself onto the landing.

Sccreeeeeek!

The fire escape swayed outward from the building. I clutched the sides tightly. A chunk of paint chipped off and tumbled to the cement below, smashing into tiny pieces.

I suddenly felt sick.

"A-Arnold?" came Max's timid voice.

"What?"

"Don't look down."

"Thanks a lot!"

I tried to focus my eyes on the fourth floor. On the vines that were still growing out of Courtney's window. Slowly I stepped down the fire escape stairs.

Sccreeeeeek! One of the steps sagged beneath my feet.

My knuckles were white. "Max, when was this thing last inspected?"

"I don't know. Listen, Arnold, if you die, can I resell your ticket to the ball game today?"

"Stop it!"

I lowered myself silently to the fourth-floor landing. I peered into Courtney's room.

Empty. Good.

I eased my fingers under her window and pulled up. With a squeak, the window rose an inch or two. Just inside, the potato was still sitting in the broken glass.

I had to blink. The potato had grown. "It's bigger!" I called upstairs. "Too big for one person to carry!"

"Could you give me an estimate in inches?"

"Get down here now, Max!"

Big mistake. The moment Max's feet hit the fire escape, it started vibrating.

"Stop that!" I warned.

"I c-c-can't h-help it." With each step, Max shuddered more. By the time he reached the fourth floor, it felt as if we were in an earthquake.

"Come on," I said, reaching my fingers under the potato. "Heave . . . ho!"

Max and I yanked hard. We barely managed to

dislodge the potato. It rolled off the windowsill and onto the fire escape, roots and all.

A thin string was wrapped around it. It pulled taut. My eyes followed it onto the floor, where it was attached to a kind of spring mechanism. The spring cocked a small hammer, which smashed down onto a black button on my old Talk-'n'-Truck Fire Engine.

"WEEE-OOOO! WEEEE-OOOO! EMER-GENCY! EMERGENCY! ALL HANDS ON DECK!" bellowed a loud recorded voice.

The bedroom door flew open. Courtney ran in, dressed in a thick terrycloth robe, her wet hair flopping down her neck.

"YOU JUVENILE DELINQUENTS! GIVE ME THAT!"

Max and I both jumped. But there was no place to jump to.

Weighed down by the potato, we fell off the landing!

12

*C*lank! Clank! Clank! Clank! Clank! Clank! Splat!

The clanks were us. The splat was the potato.

We bounced on our butts down the metal stairs and tumbled onto the third-floor landing. The potato wasn't so lucky. It rolled off the fire escape and landed on the cement in the alley below.

I thought it would smash into pieces, but it split into two equal-sized chunks.

"IF YOU TWO RUIN MY PRIZE, YOU'LL PAY!" Courtney was screaming.

Max and I clattered the rest of the way downstairs. "Brilliant idea," Max said. "Now what?"

"To the park!"

We each lifted half a potato. Throwing the vines and hairy roots over our shoulders, we ran around the front of the building.

On a Saturday morning, Olmstead Park Drive is eerily quiet. A distant lawnmower's hum and the hooting of an owl were the only sounds we heard as we carried the broken potato across the street.

The moment we made it through the entrance, I gagged.

Our burial place — our dirt patch — had been transformed.

The ground was covered with reddish-green shoots. They were spilling over each other, thick and vibrant, covering every square inch of soil.

I dropped my half-potato. "Oh no oh no oh no . . ."

"You said nothing could grow in this soil," Max remarked.

"*You* said the hormone was only activated by cooking!" I reminded him.

Max angrily threw down his half potato. "Oh, so now this is all my fault?"

"*Of course it is, you — you —*"

RRRRRRRRRRRRR . . . The lawnmower noise was becoming louder. Over a hill came a green mowing vehicle, with a sleepy-looking parks department guy in the driver's seat.

"Over here!" Max yelled, pointing frantically to the potato shoots. "Weeds! Bad, bad weeds!"

The parks guy perked up. He turned a knob on his dashboard, and the machine suddenly bucked and roared like an angry bull.

With an evil grin, he steered right for the patch. Shredded vines shot out the sides of the mower.

Red and green leaves flew left and right. Max and I kicked our potato halves under the mower. Instant pulp.

The guy mowed down the entire potato patch in even rows, leaving twisted brown stumps behind him. Max and I whooped in triumph, slapping each other high-fives.

"History!" Max hooted. "We got them all!"

I gazed over the patch, which now looked like a war zone. "Do you think they can still grow?"

Max laughed. "Are you kidding? Could *you* grow if someone scalped you like that?"

"I guess not."

Max clapped me on the shoulder. "Come on, let's have breakfast. This is the first day of vacation, and we have a ball game to go to."

Don't worry. We ate at Max's. I wouldn't dare step into our apartment after what we'd done to Courtney.

I knew Courtney was going to poison my parents' minds with her version of the story, so I called to explain. But the moment Dad picked up the phone, I could hear Courtney screeching bloody murder in the background. I decided to say that Max and I were at a pay phone in the park and were going straight to the game.

I hadn't thought about the baseball season in two days. But now that we were going, I was becoming excited. The San Dunstan Duodenums had made a lot of good trades over the winter. Max, who is the biggest Duodenums fan ever, had been keeping track of them all. He guaranteed we had a shot at first place.

The opening-day festivities were to start at eleven, but Max wanted to get there early to catch batting-practice fouls. After breakfast, around 9:30, we walked outside to the subway station, detouring past the park entrance on 96th.

The potato patch still looked chewed up. The dead shoots were wilting in the sun. Seven leashless dogs were trampling over it while their owners chatted and drank coffee.

"Success," Max said with a wink.

We ran down the subway steps, whistling "Take Me Out to the Ball Game." A few frowning passengers were straggling up, grumbling.

When we reached the bottom of the stairs, we saw why.

A big, handwritten sign on the token booth read, "Power Off." An uptown train was stuck halfway in the station. San Dunstan transit workers were on the tracks, swinging away with pickaxes.

Pickaxes?

Max and I peered over the edge of the platform. Splintered wood littered the tracks at the workers' feet. At first I thought they were hacking up the railroad ties.

But railroad ties weren't rounded. And they

didn't have long, hairy tendrils growing out of them.

"Uh-oh . . ." Max murmured.

One of the workers was crouched by the side of the lead car, busily unscrewing the metal sheet over the train's engine. He glanced at us and shook his head. "Amazing, huh? Must be the roots of some old maple tree that finally worked its way through a crack in the wall."

"Right," said Max.

"Sure," said I.

SCCRRRRAAWWWWK! The guy yanked open the sheet.

Now we could see the engine. Well, some of it. The part that wasn't covered up by thick, twisted roots.

"Well, bust my buffers . . ." the man said under his breath.

"Yo, Charlie, look at this!" another worker shouted.

He was pointing to the roof where a small crack was sending a shower of plaster onto the tracks. Through the crack, I could see a brown, dusty shape trying to emerge.

"Arnold, let's get out of here," Max said.

We flew toward the subway steps. A man and woman with a small child were heading down-ward. *"Go back!"* I yelled.

I heard a sudden, dull crack behind us.

"Yeeeeeaaagghhh!" screamed Max.

I spun around. Max was on his stomach, sliding downward, reaching out desperately to clutch the edges of the steps.

Around his ankle was a root, pulling him slowly toward the tracks!

13

"**H**E-E-E-E-ELP!" Max yelled.

I leaped down the stairs and grabbed Max's arms. I planted my legs and pulled.

It was like trying to drag a rolling car uphill. I flew over Max's head and landed on the platform.

"I got it! I got it!" shouted Charlie, the transit worker.

I looked up to see him charging toward me with an axe.

"Aaaaaaaggh!" I rolled out of the way.

Thwack! He brought the axe down, inches away from Max's ankle. It cut a big wedge into the root.

"Easy!" Max shouted hysterically. "Think about my tap-dancing career!"

Thwack! The root was broken. I raced over to help Max up while Charlie untangled the root.

The entire crew of workers was gathering around, staring at us.

"Are you okay?" I asked.

"Terrific," Max said. "My ankle's practically broken, and a potato almost dragged me to my death, but other than that, I haven't felt better in my life."

"Potato?" said one of the workers with a laugh.

"Looks like an oak to me," said another.

"Nahhh, sycamore . . ."

"I knew this would happen," said a grizzled, gray-haired worker. "The system's falling apart. You got your roots, your pipes, your cables, all squidged together . . ."

"Gah —" Max grunted, pointing upstairs, his eyes wide as tennis balls.

I looked up. Through small cracks in the stairway wall, more roots were emerging. Slowly they were coiling onto the stairs, slithering down toward us.

Beep-beep! went an alarm on the old guy's watch. "Coffee break!" he announced.

I managed to unclench my throat. "*Run!*"

Max and I bolted back down the stairs, onto the platform.

The workers were heading in the other direction, thermoses in hand, chattering away. The vines slithered behind them, curling onto the tracks.

"To the end of the station!" Max yelled. "We can use the stairs there!"

We raced toward the exit at the Ninety-seventh Street side.

Crrrrrack! Crrrrrack! Crrrrrack!

Roots burst up from the stairs themselves, waving like monstrous earthworms.

We were trapped at the edge of the station now. Roots were sliding toward us from all directions but one.

The tunnel.

I leaned over the platform and looked uptown. The tunnel was dark and strewn with litter. Every few feet, a bare lightbulb illuminated jagged graffiti on the grimy walls. A river of filthy black water trickled between the tracks.

Never. Not for all the money in the world would I step into a place like that. I'd rather go through the Tunnel of Love with Deena Blodgett.

"Watch it!" Max shouted.

I felt a potato root tickling my ankle.

"Come on!" I said, jumping onto the tracks.

Max looked horrified. "Oh, sure. I love stepping on dead animals and electrocuting myself on the third rail!"

"The power's off! Didn't you read the sign?"

A root burst through the wall next to Max. He screamed and hopped onto the track.

We ran into the dark tunnel. Our feet splashed in the muck.

"This is disgusting!" Max said. "What if I step on a rat?"

"You can't!" I called over my shoulder. "The ones down here come up to your knees!"

"Thanks for telling me!"

BBBBBBRROMMMMMM!

The noise shook the entire tunnel. Max and I nearly tumbled off our feet.

"What was that?" Max yelled.

From behind us, I heard a deep, loud, rumbling sound. "A train?" I guessed.

"I thought you said the power was off!"

I turned and looked into the semi-darkness. About fifty yards away, I could make out a hole in the roof. Wires and pipes dangled down from it in a cloud of plaster dust.

Through the dust, a shape lumbered down the track toward us. A large shape, the size of a subway train.

But it was clearly not a train. Not at all.

Trains weren't round. Trains didn't have torn roots hanging from them.

We were about to be flattened — by a potato!

14

"*G*O-O-O-O-O!*" I ran into Max and fell. The two of us tumbled onto the track. I could feel soft, squishy things beneath me.

Max sprang to his feet and grabbed my arm. "COME ON!"

I staggered upward and ran.

The potato was picking up speed. It was pushing the air through the tunnel, creating a wind at our backs. The ground shook violently. Max yelled something to me, but the noise was so loud I couldn't hear him.

"WHAAAAAAAT?" I shouted.

"*I SAID,*" Max bellowed at the top of his lungs, "*DON'T LOOK BACK!*"

I looked back. The potato was gaining on us, rolling over its own broken roots. Its bumps and knobs looked like moon craters.

"*AAAAAAAAAAA!*"

My legs pounded the tracks. I could see small

creatures skittering for cover, but I didn't care. Max and I were booking.

We sprinted around a curve. About a hundred yards ahead of us was the dim yellow light of the 103rd Street station.

RRRRRRRRRRRRROMMMMMMM!

The odor of potato was overpowering now. I could practically taste the soil and mildew.

Closer . . . closer . . . I was running out of breath. My legs were killing me, screaming at me to slow down.

Thwack! The spinning tip of a root whipped against my back.

In the station, three teenage kids with backward-turned baseball caps were leaning over the platform, gawking at us.

"GIVE US A HAND!" Max yelled.

The kids nodded approvingly and started to clap.

Max reached the station first. He grabbed onto a ladder at the edge of the platform and hopped up.

Thwack-thwack-thwack-thwack. The roots were pelting me now. I lunged for the ladder.

My fingertips latched onto the top rung — for a moment. Then they slipped.

Screaming, I fell to the tracks!

15

"**G**otcha!"

I felt a hand close over my right wrist. And then I was hurtling up onto the cement platform, head over heels.

When I stopped, I was all tangled up with Max.

"We have to . . . stop . . . meeting like this," Max said, gulping for air.

The potato rolled into the station and thudded to a stop, trapped between the platform and the wall.

"Cooool," said the three kids in unison, gathering around the potato.

A bleary-looking man in a long coat walked up to us. "Uh, excuse me," he said. "Is this an uptown potato or a downtown potato?"

"Uptown," Max said. "But don't —"

"Thanks," the man replied, rushing toward the downtown steps.

I took Max by the arm. "Let's get out of here!"

As we raced upstairs, I took one last look at the three kids.

They were decorating the potato with graffiti.

Max and I emerged back up into the sunny spring morning. The smell of city air was like a cool, refreshing drink. Outside a corner drugstore, we paused to catch our breaths.

"You — you saved my life, Max," I said.

"Remember that, next time you want to blame me for everything."

"You boys having a little problem?" a rough voice called.

I turned to see a tall policeman at the curb. He had a face like a pit bull in a bad mood. He was in the middle of writing a ticket for a parked car.

We both ran to him. "Am I glad to see you!" I said. "My friend Max and I? We were going to a ball game, but Max was dragged into the station by a root? Anyway, we jumped onto the track and started running, and this potato chased us all the way to One-hundred-third Street."

The cop was eyeing our clothing. "I suppose that explains the getup."

I looked down at myself. My sweats were practically black with soot. Wet newspapers clung to my pants, along with three wads of old bubblegum, two candy wrappers, and an orange peel.

Max didn't look any better. "Officer," he said, "you don't happen to have a change of clothes at the station, do you? Large T-shirt, waist twenty-six pants and underwear, preferably boxers?"

The policeman heaved a sigh and took out his walkie-talkie. "Patrolman Guernsey here," he said into the receiver. "I have two runaways on One-hundred-third and Olmstead Park Drive. I'll bring them in."

"*Runaways?*" Max exclaimed. "Wait! You don't understand —"

"Yeah, yeah. You can tell the nice chief all about the big tomatoes."

"Potatoes!" Max protested.

"Them, too. Now, hang on while I finish."

Officer Guernsey continued writing out the parking ticket he'd started.

The car was a dilapidated old Chevy parked a few feet beyond a sign that read NO PARKING FROM HERE TO CORNER.

A young woman came dashing around the corner, carrying two grocery bags. "Excuse me, officer, that's mine!"

Officer Guernsey ripped out the completed ticket and stuck it under the windshield wiper. "Too late, ma'am, it's already written."

"But it's Saturday —" the woman pleaded.

"Doesn't matter. The car is on *this* side of the sign. If it were on the *other* side —"

BBOOOOOOOOMMMMM!

The street shook. In the drugstore window,

glass shelves full of vitamin bottles crashed to the floor.

A crack formed in the middle of the road, shooting chunks of soil and asphalt into the air. It quickly widened, then began to spread toward us.

Officer Guernsey's mouth dropped open so fast, it nearly clanked against his badge.

Encrusted with dirt, the top of a root emerged from the street. It ripped open the pavement as if it were a thin pie crust, and traveled under the parked car, lifting it off the street.

"My car!" the woman screamed.

The root pushed forward, moving the car with it. Then it veered to the right and disappeared underground again.

With a loud *whomp*, the car landed on all four tires. It was now about fifteen feet behind the place it had been before. Just outside the No Parking zone.

Officer Guernsey looked about ten years older. He took the ticket from the windshield and tore it up. "Violation removed," he said, his voice a parched whisper. "And I think you boys have a lot of explaining to do at the station house . . ."

16

"Spilling out of the dishwasher . . ." Police Chief Crenshaw repeated, scribbling in a spiral notebook.

"Right, and the sink," I said. "So at first we thought the hormone only worked when it was heated up."

"Of course," Chief Crenshaw said.

"Then I saw the vines in my window," Max cut in, "so we tried to steal Courtney's potato but she booby-trapped her room with prune juice, so we snuck down the fire escape to steal it but it was too heavy and it fell, so we took the pieces to the park and got the lawnmower guy to smash them while he cut down the shoots —"

"But when we went into the subway," I went on, "we saw roots breaking through the wall so we ran onto the track, where the giant potato chased us here."

"Uh-huh," Chief Crenshaw said, still writing. "And where is the potato in question?"

"In the station, covered with graffiti."

Chief Crenshaw dropped his pencil and buried his face in his hands. I peeked over the top of the desk and saw that he had been sketching Bugs Bunny and the Road Runner.

He hadn't been taking us seriously at all!

I shifted uncomfortably in a green plastic chair. I was feeling queasy and claustrophobic. The windows in Chief Crenshaw's office were grimy brown, and the air smelled like old cigarette smoke and bad breath.

"Look, fellas," Chief Crenshaw said, "I'm going to order us some food, while you guys change into clothes from the charity boxes inside. Then I'll send you home for a little R and R. Sure, you may have differences with your parents, but it's a rough world out there —"

"We're not runaways, sir!" I said. "Don't you believe us? The whole city is in danger. Ask Officer Guernsey!" I spun around. "Where is he, anyway?"

"Suspended for ripping up a parking ticket." Chief Crenshaw leaned forward, fixing a level stare at me. "He set you up, didn't he? Couldn't you guys have thought of a better excuse?"

"But — but it's not —" I began to protest.

"Williams!" Chief Crenshaw called into his intercom. "Call Burgers 'n' Stuff over on Ninety-seventh Street and order me a triple baconcheeseburger, two hot dogs with sauerkraut, a large fries, a box of assorted donuts, two chocolate shakes, a black coffee, and . . ." He turned from the speaker. "What do you boys want?"

Useless. I sank back in my chair.

Max and I each ordered a shake. We'd lost our appetites in the tunnel. While we waited for the delivery, Chief Crenshaw picked out clothes for us from charity donations that were kept in the next room.

Talk about cruel. The plaid pants and polyester Hawaiian shirt he gave me were a terrible fit. But Max's ripped woolen knickers and extra-large turtleneck looked worse, so I couldn't complain.

The food arrived soon afterward, in three big brown-paper bags. Chief Crenshaw tore open the first one. Fries spilled over the top of the bag as he pulled out a foil-wrapped burger. "Yum . . . and here's my coffee . . ." As he lifted a small cardboard cup, the top fell off, revealing about a dozen soggy fries inside.

Max opened another bag. It ripped down the side, and fries cascaded onto the table.

I took a greasy box of donuts out of the third bag. When I opened it, I realized what had caused the grease.

It wasn't the donuts.

You guessed it. Fries were everywhere — in the holes, on the chocolate frosting, even sticking out of the crullers.

My stomach was sinking.

"I'm not seeing this," Max murmured.

"What's going on here?" Chief Crenshaw grumbled. He hit the intercom button and barked, "Williams! Get Burgers 'n' Stuff on the phone!"

A moment later Chief Crenshaw's phone lit up. He yanked up the receiver and shouted, "Crenshaw here. You went a little heavy on the fries, pal — what? . . . What on earth are you talking about, 'a portion control problem with the potatoes'? Get me the manager!"

"Portion-control problem?" Max and I said at the same time.

Out of the corner of my eye I spotted another phone extension, near a window. "I'll gather intelligence," I said. "You isolate the spuds!"

Max frantically picked the fries out of the food and dumped them into an empty waste barrel. I snatched up the phone extension and interrupted Chief Crenshaw's conversation. "Hello, Burgers 'n' Stuff? This is Deputy Mayhew. Tell me where you got the potatoes for your french fries, or it's the slammer for you, buddy."

Chief Crenshaw looked flabbergasted. "Wha — hey, you —"

Max quickly brushed his hand across the table, knocking the cup of coffee onto Chief Crenshaw's shiny black shoes.

"Yaaah!" the chief dropped the phone and jumped out of his seat.

"So sorry, my mistake," Max said, grabbing a

fistful of tissues from the chief's desk. "Let me clean it up."

Perfect distraction.

"Well, sir," the voice at the other end of the phone line was saying. "I was walking to work through the park this morning, when I spotted a patch of gorgeous potatoes, right in Olmstead Park. I figured, hey, why not?"

"How many did you pick?" I shouted.

"Just one, sir. Two boys were heading into the park, so I pocketed it and left . . . "

I had a horrible sinking feeling. *"How many people have eaten the french fries?"*

"No one. The workers all fled, saying the potatoes were multiplying. That scared the customers, and — oops, someone's at the office door. *Come in!* As I was saying . . . Oh, dear. Oh, my goodness. How did they . . . ? *Yiiiiii!"*

The phone went dead.

I slammed the receiver down.

"The spuds have attacked the burger place!" I shouted to Max.

I leaped to the chief's desk and scooped the remaining fries into the barrel.

The bathroom was just outside the office door, near the exit. I ran in and began dumping the fries into the toilet.

"What do you think you're doing?" Chief Crenshaw roared.

"Saving your life!" I replied.

76

He was going to catch me. I knew it. Racing against time, I dumped and flushed, dumped and flushed . . .

I heard crashing and yelling from the office. I didn't know what was happening. I just hoped Max was still alive.

FOOOOOSH! Down went the last of the fries.

A hand landed on my collar. My life flashed before me.

"Come on, quick!"

It was Max. "How — what — ?"

I glanced into the office. Chief Crenshaw was sitting on the floor, trying to unknot his shoelaces, which had been tied together. *"WIIIIILI-AAAAMS!"* he shouted.

My feet have never moved so fast. We were on the street in a nanosecond.

RRRRRRAAAAAAWWWWWRRRR . . .

Judging from the number of sirens, so was the entire San Dunstan police force!

17

"**P**laying for the Duodenums ... ums ...
ums ... " echoed the voice of the San Dunstan stadium announcer.

I scanned exits. I counted at least six police uniforms.

"*In center field ... ield ... ield ...* "

"Do you think they'll find us here?" I whispered
to Max.

Max raised a how-can-you-be-so-stupid eye-
brow. "Sure. Two totally average twelve-year-old
guys in a crowd of forty thousand."

He was right. We were completely unnotice-
able. To hide our weird outfits, we had bought San
Dunstan Duodenums T-shirts, and our programs
were unfolded on our laps.

"*Rrrrrralph Rrrrrrackstraw!*" the announcer
bellowed.

I sat back and tried to relax. "Max? How'd this
team get its name? I thought the duodenum was
part of the intestine."

Max nodded. "It is. The team owner thought it was the name of a Greek god."

"Cre-e-enshaw, got 'em!"

I leaped out of my seat with a gasp.

A vendor was walking up the aisle, holding two boxes aloft. "Ge-e-et your popcorn!"

Easy, Mayhew, I said to myself. *You're hearing things.*

I was a total train wreck. I could barely focus on the game.

Which was just as well, because the Duodenums' opponents loaded the bases with two outs in the top of the first.

That was when another vendor's cry made my blood run cold:

"Fries here!"

"Fries?" I squeaked.

There they were. Coming up the stairs. Drooping greasily out of paper bags.

"Get them out of here!" I blurted out.

The vendor gave me a nasty look and kept walking.

"Arnold, I'm worried about you," Max said.

"Worried about me?" I shot back. "Worry about San Dunstan, Max! While we're sitting here, our potatoes are ripping up the streets. Attacking fast-food managers. All because of the stupid tube with the cube —"

Max stood up from his seat. "There you go again! Always passing the blame. Always me, me, me! I don't remember *you* stopping me at the lab —"

Smmmmack!

At the crack of a bat, the crowd fell silent. Max and I turned to see a baseball rising into the outfield.

The center fielder Ralph Rackstraw raced after it, deep into the outfield grass.

"Auuugghh, it's going over his head!" Max said.

The ball was way deep. It had grand slam written all over it. The crowd was on its feet. The entire stadium seemed to be rumbling. Rackstraw was almost to the warning track . . .

Suddenly it seemed as if he were running uphill. The ground beneath him was rising.

Just before he reached the fence, he was catapulted straight upward. As if on a trampoline, he sailed above the top of the fence . . . above the scoreboard . . .

He stabbed his mitt high. At the 12 of the scoreboard clock, the ball smacked into his palm.

Even from our seats in the bleachers, I could see the strange look of joy and fear on Rackstraw's face.

Clutching the ball tightly, he fell.

He landed on the top of the huge brown object that had broken through the ground to launch him.

An object the size of a school bus.

In the stunned silence that followed, the announcer's voice blared out shakily:

"Interference . . . by a potato?"

18

The place was going nuts. Brawls broke out on the field. Half of the crowd was racing for the exits, half was laughing uncontrollably.

"*It's happening, Max! You see?*" I shouted. "*They're taking over!*"

The aisles were full of policemen now. They were shouting into walkie-talkies and scanning the stands through binoculars.

"*Now the cops are coming for us!*"

"Chill, Arnold!"

"*Nobody says chill anymore!*"

"Quick, look like a grown-up!"

He jutted out his belly, pressed his chin against his neck and waddled out. I imitated him. I felt like a complete idiot.

A nervous, hysterical idiot.

We were nearly trampled by the crowd, but we managed to make our way to the street.

"Where to now?" Max shouted.

"A plane to Mexico might be nice!" I shouted back.

"How about home?"

"Close enough!"

We ran through the parking lot and onto Duodenum Field Road. We made tracks across the lawn of the San Dunstan Performing Arts Center and cut across San Dunstan Civic Plaza.

My legs ached. My lungs felt ripped apart. By the plaza water fountain, I stopped short. "Hold it, Max!"

Gulping for breath, I reached into the cool, clear water and rinsed my face. Above me, an enormous statue of the city's founding family, the Dunstans, squirted water out of their mouths and fingertips. It is the world's ugliest sculpture, but boy, was I grateful for the refreshment.

I dug in again. I noticed a few leaves came along with this handful, but no matter. They were cool, too.

Then I noticed something odd. The sound of the trickling water had stopped.

"Oh no . . . " Max was whispering.

I looked up. The Dunstans were no longer dribbling water. They were spitting leaves. Red and green leaves.

My feet barely touched the ground. Max and I were flying.

Near a large apartment building on Curry

Street, we hit a rain squall. "We should have brought umbrellas!" I shouted.

Max stopped. "This is weird, Arnold. It's sunny and clear."

"Don't stop! It's only a sun shower —"

"On one side of the street?" He gestured to the opposite sidewalk, which was totally dry.

We looked upward. On all the big buildings in San Dunstan are cylindrical wooden water tanks, which supply the building's water. The one above us was pouring. It had been shattered. By something that had grown inside it.

And you can guess what.

All around us, people were screaming. Cars screeched to a stop. Gawkers piled out of storefronts.

"They've taken over the water system!" I cried out, sprinting toward home. "How'd they get in there?"

"*You flushed those french fries!*" Max retorted.

Tahiti. Bermuda. Auckland. I thought of places my family could escape to. The minute I arrived home, I was going to make Mom and Dad buy plane tickets. To a place over the ocean. To a place where I knew the potatoes wouldn't follow.

Maybe Antarctica.

We turned down Olmstead Park Drive. We passed Ninety-eighth Street ... Ninety-seventh ...

As we approached Ninety-sixth, I noticed the

subway entrance. It was covered with so many vines, it looked like a jungle rising out of the sidewalk. The buckling street had been closed off to traffic with police barricades.

Police barricades!

I tried to stop short at the corner of Ninety-sixth Street, but I was going too fast. Max and I both shot around at top speed.

Right into a throng of people in front of my building.

In the center, grinning triumphantly, was Chief Crenshaw!

19

"**A**rnold!" yelled Mom and Dad.

"Max!" yelled Mr. and Mrs. Beekly.

"Get them!" bellowed Chief Crenshaw through a bullhorn.

Three cops raced toward us. A TV camera van skidded to a stop at the curb.

"Quick!" Max said, pulling his Duodenums T-shirt up so it covered his head. "Do the perp walk!"

"The what?"

"You know, like on the nightly news? Whenever the cops catch perpetrators and walk them in front of the TV cameras? The dudes are always covering their faces!"

I pulled my shirt up, too. The next thing I knew, strong fingers closed around my arm and pushed me forward.

"We're here at Ninety-sixth Street," a newswoman was saying, "with the two young men who, sources say, may be the twisted masterminds be-hind the outbreak of mutant tubers uptown . . . "

"Cut!" another voice called out. "Excuse me, perps? Can you lower your heads a bit, and drag your feet instead of bounce? And officer, slow the walk down! And tuck in your shirt, please. Thank you. Okay, roll 'em!"

The newswoman started her lines again.

"This is cool," I heard Max say.

Cool? Visions of rock piles and ankle chains were dancing in my head.

I could hear my parents and the Beeklys argu-ing with Chief Crenshaw. But as we drew closer, he asked someone, "Is the camera on? How's my hair?"

I felt myself being turned around. Looking down, all I could see under the shirt was a section of the sidewalk. I recognized Chief Crenshaw's shoes. "Thought you could escape, huh?" Chief Crenshaw muttered. Then he cleared his throat and announced, "Ladies and gentlemen, this is one bright moment in a dark, dark day for the city of San Dunstan. Don't be fooled by the small size of these young men. I have met them, and they are dangerous."

"I can explain everything!" I heard Mom cry out in the background.

Chief Crenshaw ignored her. " . . . And I urge all citizens not to panic," he went on. "The police department is doing all in its power to get to the root of this problem and, er, stem it . . . "

"What are you going to do?" someone called out from the crowd behind us. "Arrest the potatoes?"

"Er . . . uh . . . harrumph," Chief Crenshaw said. "We are studying the options . . . "

A sudden movement caught my eye. A worm-like, slithering movement.

A vine crept across the sidewalk, inches from my foot.

I took a quick step back. The vine's tip touched Chief Crenshaw's shoe, then detoured around his heel. Slowly it twined upward, circling his ankle . . . his calf . . .

" . . . Our officers are working with the pest control department —" Chief Crenshaw broke off in midsentence. He let go of my arm. He was trying to pull his leg free, but the vine only grabbed tighter. "HE-E-E-ELLLLP!"

20

"**R**un, Max!" I yanked my shirt down and bolted.

"Go upstairs!" my dad shouted. "You'll be safe there! Take Courtney!"

Max and I plowed through the panicking throng. Courtney was already behind us. "I hope you're happy now, Arnold," she said. "Destroying the city at age twelve. What'll you do next?"

"Courtney, don't you ever stop?" I asked.

When we reached the front door, we dashed into the lobby. Another vine was sliding in behind us, following the base of the wall.

"Back! Back!" Courtney yelled to the vine. "Take the two traitors. I come in peace!"

I pressed the elevator button and the door opened. Max and I ran in.

"Come on!" I called out.

Courtney jumped in, and we all rode up to the fourth floor. "I hope you have a plan to stop all this," she said.

89

"I didn't plan for any of this to start!"

"You couldn't just let me do my science fair project," Courtney barreled on. "You just had to outdo me. You had to go steal the hormone, and look what happened. Now what am I going to do? 'How Mold Forms on Bread'?"

"Courtney, stop worrying about your dumb project!" Max said. "At this rate you won't even have a school to do it in!"

I let us all into the apartment and slammed the door behind us.

WEEE-OOOO-WEEE-OOOO-WEEE-OOOO! a siren sounded from outside.

Max, Courtney, and I ran to the living room window and looked out. Below us was a real mess. People were running all over the place. A fire engine was weaving down the street, bouncing over all the vines that had popped through the pavement.

A firefighter hopped off the truck, grabbed an ax, and began chopping the vine that had trapped Chief Crenshaw.

"Oh, great," I said. "As soon as Crenshaw is loose, we're hamburger."

We all started pacing. "What now?" Max asked.

"We could call a taxi," I suggested.

"A helicopter," Max said.

"A restaurant," Courtney chimed in.

"How can you be hungry at a time like this?" I asked.

Ding-dong!

I ran for the door. "That must be Mom and Dad!"

"Don't open it!" Max warned. "What if it's the cops?"

I peered through the front door peephole. Two men were standing there, wearing tall chef's hats. "Who is it?"

"Pizza?" a gruff voice called out.

"This guy sounds familiar," Max said.

Courtney was smiling. "They must have ESP!"

"Nobody ordered pizza here!" I said loudly.

"Want it anyway?" the guy asked. "The people who ordered it aren't home."

"Sure!" Courtney cried out.

"Any potatoes on it?" Max asked.

"Nahhhh, pepperoni."

"I *love* pepperoni!" Courtney exclaimed, pulling open the door.

The two men stepped inside. One of them looked more like a college professor than a pizza guy. He had thick glasses and a small chin, and he was carrying a black leather bag. The other was shorter, with dark eyes and a beard stubble. He was wearing a green industrial-looking uniform with the initials SDMNH on the front pocket.

"Uh, where's the pie?" Max asked.

The uniformed guy shut the door behind him. "We need to collect a small payment first."

"I have my mom's credit card!" Courtney offered.

I was trying to figure out what SDMNH meant. San Dunstan something . . .

The other man spoke up. "We don't take credit."

That voice. I knew it . . .

"San Dunstan Museum of Natural History!" I blurted out. "That's what the letters stand for!"

The shorter guy grinned. "Give this boy a prize, Dr. Nardo."

"Why should I, Ralphie?" the other one replied, taking a step toward me. "He already stole mine."

21

The two men walked slowly toward us. Courtney, Max, and I backed into the living room.

"Let me warn you now," Max said. "They have a fierce killer dog here!"

"Who, *Yappy*?" Courtney said.

"Here, Yappy!" I called out. "Yappy!"

Typical. At the least sign of danger, Yappy likes to hide in the closet.

"Did you think you could get away with this?" Dr. Nardo asked. "The security guard gave us a perfect description and even told us who your mom was. This is a serious crime, kids."

"Any more serious than your theft?" Max asked. "Stealing the mosquito in amber from a dig site that belongs to the museum?"

Dr. Nardo's face flinched. "How do you know — ?"

"Never mind!" Ralphie snapped. "Just give us the test tube."

"We can't!" Max replied.

"You must have replicated gallons of it!" Dr. Nardo said. "Judging from all the unusual growth activity outside."

"Replicated it?" I said. "We're only twelve years old!"

"We don't even know what replicate means!" Max added.

"Don't play dumb with us!" Ralphie growled.

"WAIT A MINUTE!" Courtney yelled. "Let me get this straight. You mean, you guys *didn't* bring a pizza?"

"Drop it, Courtney!" Max said.

Courtney marched off toward the kitchen. "Well, then, *I'm* going to order some myself!"

"Hey!" Dr. Nardo shouted, stepping toward her.

"I'll get her!" Ralphie cried.

I did the first thing that popped into my mind.

I rammed my shoulder into Dr. Nardo.

"Gahhh!" He fell backward, knocking over Ralphie.

"*Let's go!*" I shouted.

Max bolted for the door. I darted toward Courtney, grabbed her hand, and ran after him.

"ARNOLD GET YOUR COOTIES OFF ME!" Courtney protested.

We both stumbled out in the hallway. Courtney was trying to pull loose.

Max was standing nervously by the elevator, ramming the down button. "*Hurry!*" he called out.

"Take the stairs!" I said.

Our apartment door banged open. "Not so fast!" yelled Dr. Nardo.

He and Ralphie flew toward us. They stood in front of the door, red-faced with fury.

Dr. Nardo was fishing around in his black bag. "I have something here that may persuade you to tell the truth . . . "

The elevator door slid open.

So did my jaw.

Behind the two men, like a strange piece of elevator furniture, was a six-foot-tall potato!

Its tendrils reached around Ralphie and Dr. Nardo.

"Hey —"

"What —"

The two men went white with shock. They kicked wildly as they were dragged backward into the elevator.

"*Helllp!*" Dr. Nardo yelled.

I seized his hand. "I've got you!"

"ARNOLD, WHAT ARE YOU DOING?" Courtney screamed, grabbing my hand. "THEY'RE THE BAD GUYS!"

"Come back!" Max cried, pulling Courtney.

"AAAAAAAGGGHHHHHH!" shouted Ralphie.

I tried to lock my legs but I couldn't. The potato yanked us all into the elevator. We fell to the floor.

With a whoosh, the door closed behind us.

22

"**W**E'RE GOING TO DIE!" Courtney cried. More vines were shooting out from the potato, wrapping around all of us, like a big, horrible bear hug.

"*Why couldn't they be friendly?*" Max said through gritted teeth.

The elevator wasn't moving. The 4 on the overhead strip was brightly lit. Courtney was near the control panel, shrieking so loud I could barely think.

The vine was now tightening around my chest. I was short of breath. I was beginning to see stars. Everything was fading from sight — the potato, the two men, Max and Courtney, the control panel . . .

An idea seeped into my half-conscious brain.

"*Courtney!*" I gasped. "*Hit . . . the . . . top . . . floor . . . button!*"

"I'M TOO YOUNG TO —" Courtney blared.

Max spun around. Pinned to the potato, he could walk his feet up the elevator wall.

With a sharp kick, he struck 12, the top floor.

The elevator didn't move. The potato began to shake.

Then, slowly, I felt us rise. The tendrils were loosening now. The potato seemed to be compressing against the floor.

Then, with a sudden *snnnnnnap*, we shot upward.

All four of us fell. The tendrils hung limply around us.

"What happened?" Courtney asked.

I had to gulp for air. "We . . . we snapped . . . the root."

Dr. Nardo was looking at me with awe. "Brilliant!"

"You saved our lives!" Ralphie exclaimed.

Courtney smiled. "Maybe you're not so useless after all, Arnold."

"Thanks, guys," I said.

"Yo, how about some praise for the kicker?" Max said.

The doors opened at the top floor.

Dr. Nardo jumped to his feet. "Out. Everybody."

"So, I guess you're not mad at us anymore?" I asked.

Dr. Nardo and Ralphie exchanged a look. Ralphie pulled the elevator's emergency stop button. A shrill alarm rang out.

"What'd you do that for?" Max asked.

"So it'll be here when we return," Dr. Nardo replied.

"Let's work together, Dr. Nardo," I said over the noise. "You're a scientist. Maybe you can help us find a way to destroy the potatoes. Imagine the headlines — Ralphie and Nardo save the city!"

The two men led us to the door that said ROOF. "Climb," Dr. Nardo commanded.

We all walked up and onto the roof. As we shut the door behind us, the clanging of the elevator alarm was cut off. Below us the city sounded oddly muffled. The potatoes must have blocked all traffic to the neighborhood.

"So, you want me to save the city?" With a grin, Dr. Nardo reached into his black bag and pulled out a long syringe with thin leather strips hanging from it.

"I'm going to faint," Courtney said.

Dr. Nardo chuckled. "Not to worry. Here, in this syringe with a fringe, is a fluid developed from a common coenzyme inhibitor that blocks the electron transport chain of organisms with abnormally high growth rates."

We all stared at him in a big group Duh.

"In other words," Dr. Nardo said, "inject this into the potatoes, and they can't breathe. They shrivel up and die. The effect causes a chain reaction throughout the entire root."

"All riiiiight!" I exclaimed.

"Well, go ahead, Nardo babes!" Max said.

"Not so fast." Dr. Nardo smiled. "I think you kids should have the glory of killing the potatoes — before the press and the police, of course. You'll be heroes."

"Yyyyes!" Courtney said, reaching for the syringe. "I could write *this* up for the science fair!"

"But first," Dr. Nardo said, "you give us back the growth hormone."

I swallowed hard. "Well, we would if we could . . . "

"But we used it all up," Max admitted.

I thought Dr. Nardo was going to explode. *"Whaaat?"*

"They're lying!" Ralphie growled.

The two men began stepping slowly toward us.

"If I don't hear where the rest of the hormone is in, oh, ten seconds," Dr. Nardo said, reaching into his black bag, "you two are in for a very long flight down . . . "

We shuffled backward, closer and closer to the edge of the roof!

"Stop!" Max shouted. "It's . . . it's in my bedroom!"

I gave him a look. "It is?"

Max bowed his head. "I admit it. I kept part of it, after all."

"But how — ?" I began.

"Where's your bedroom?" Ralphie demanded.

Max dug his keys out of his pocket. "These'll get you into apartment 5E. Follow your nose the rest

99

of the way. You'll find the precious potion in the box full of socks, near the sink with the ink, on the dresser for the . . . uh . . . uh . . . "

Dr. Nardo's face fell.

Ralphie began slamming his right fist into his left palm. "You mock us!" he said, stepping forward again.

"Mock?" Max squeaked. "Me? Mock?"

"What a shame," Dr. Nardo said. "You seemed like such nice kids . . . "

Back we went . . . back toward the edge . . .

"The cops are probably on the way up, you know!" I said.

"They'll have to climb twelve flights," Dr. Nardo said, "because the elevator is stuck. Besides, I'll tell them the truth. I was merely trying to retrieve the growth hormone and you all had a . . . mishap, trying to keep it from me. Do you think they'll doubt the word of a world-renowned scientist?"

We were at the very edge. I looked around. A tiny ledge of cement separated us from a twelve-story fall.

"You can't do this!" Max said.

"Oh, no?" Dr. Nardo and Ralphie held up their arms, palms out. "Watch."

23

"*I HAVE IT!*" Courtney suddenly pulled a glass tube from her jacket pocket.

"We heard that one already, sister!" Ralphie said.

"Wait! Let me see that!" Dr. Nardo said.

Grumbling, Ralphie backed off.

Dr. Nardo took the tube. A yellow happy-face label was glued to it. "Where did you get this?"

Courtney was trembling. "After Arnold told me he stole the growth hormone, I mentioned it to my mom. At first she acted shocked. Then she said that she knew all about it. She saw you take the mosquito in the amber, Dr. Nardo. Ever since, she's been keeping track of you, and she'd overheard you talking about the hormone. She knew about the two samples — in the tube with the cube and the vial with the smile."

"The vial with the smile?" Ralphie repeated.

Dr. Nardo swallowed hard. "No, this isn't it. Not the vial with the smile. It's the jar with the star!"

"*What?*" Ralphie's eyes were blazing. "You said you were giving *me* the only sample!"

"Well, you see, Ralphie, it's like this . . . " Dr. Nardo began.

As he blabbered on, I could see a vine crawling up over the ledge of the building — heading right for Courtney!

"Watch it!" I warned.

Courtney leaped away. She snatched the syringe out of Dr. Nardo's hand.

"Hey!" Dr. Nardo shouted.

He and Ralphie both pounced. They grabbed Courtney's hand, turning the syringe toward her.

Max and I leaped on the two men, but they were strong as bulls.

"NO!" Courtney screamed, as the needle came closer and closer to her face. "NO-O-O-O-O!"

24

"**F**r — fr — freeze!"

We all looked left, toward the voice.

Over the fire escape stepped Chief Crenshaw, panting for breath.

Courtney bared her teeth and dug them into Dr. Nardo's forearm.

"YEEEOOW!" Dr. Nardo's palm opened up. The syringe went flying.

"*Catch that!*" I yelled.

Max, Courtney, and I dived for it at the same time. The needle was pointing downward.

We yanked our hands away.

The syringe smashed to the ground, shattering into a million pieces.

"Oh, nooo!" Courtney moaned.

"Officer," Dr. Nardo said, "in the name of the San Dunstan Museum of Natural History, arrest those kids!"

A whole team of cops was now climbing over the

rooftop. Chief Crenshaw was limping in our direction, holding handcuffs.

I held out my hands and stifled a sob. What was the difference now? I'd only be in jail a short time. Soon the whole city would be destroyed.

Chief Crenshaw turned. With a quick, sharp movement, he slapped the cuffs onto the wrists of Dr. Nardo and Ralphie.

"Wha — who — " Dr. Nardo sputtered. "Do you know who you are harrassing?"

"I sure do," Chief Crenshaw said. "And you're under arrest — for theft of sensitive scientific property. I got the whole story from Dr. Mayhew downstairs, pal. She told me about everything in that lab of yours. I radioed a team of officers to raid it, and they should be here any minute."

The vine was now creeping over the ledge, right for Chief Crenshaw. "Watch out!" I said.

"Aaagh!" Chief Crenshaw stepped quickly away.

From all sides of the apartment building, more vines slapped onto the rooftop and slowly slithered inward.

"Any bright ideas about this one, Nardo?" Ralphie asked.

Dr. Nardo cackled. "Arrest us, Crenshaw, and you still have a major problem on your hands. The antidote is all over the floor — at least *this* sample is. Let me go, and perhaps we can work out a deal for the rest."

Ralphie glowered at Dr. Nardo. *"You've got more of that stuff, too?"*

"No, *we* do!" a familiar voice called out.

"Mom?" Courtney and I said at the same time.

Over the rooftop climbed my mother. She ran to us and we threw our arms around her.

Behind her was another team of cops, spilling onto the roof and sprinting toward us.

When I saw what they were holding, I had to rub my eyes.

"I don't believe this," Max muttered.

"Yahoo!" Courtney cheered.

In the hand of each cop was a syringe with a dangling leather fringe.

"This is — burglary!" Dr. Nardo sputtered. "Breaking and entering — disruption of the scientific process — "

Chief Crenshaw pushed him and Ralphie toward the roof door. "Yeah, yeah, tell it to each other in the clink!"

As they disappeared inside, the cops ran to the vines and pushed the antidote into each.

One by one, the vines began to wither and die.

"Yyyyyyyes!" I shouted. I felt as if a cement block had been lifted from my shoulder.

Max and I whooped and hollered like two monkeys. Finally the nightmare was over. The potatoes were on the run. The city was safe.

"Will it work for them all?" Courtney asked.

Mom nodded. "I believe the roots are all at-

tached. This stuff will travel the entire length —
and if Dr. Nardo's supply is not enough, we can
learn how to manufacture more."

"That's it! *That's* my science fair project!"
Courtney said. Then she looked at me and Max
with concern. "Unless you guys want to do it."

"Uh, no thanks, Courtney," I said. "I think I'll
stick to S'mores."

Epilogue

"So," Dad said, walking out of Courtney's room toward the kitchen, "what shall we have for dinner?"

Courtney, Max, Mom, and I were picking up potato vine leaves and broken glass from Courtney's floor. It had been a long day. After giving a police report, we'd all gone to the museum. There, Mom found the jar with the star in Dr. Nardo's lab, plus another sample of the growth hormone in a jug on a rug. She's already planning to start a study committee. (Nobel Prize, here we come.)

"After a day like today," I said, "let's celebrate with something cool, like ice cream with pudding and Cool Whip!"

"Nahhh," said Max. "Potato dumplings."

"Home fries," Mom suggested.

"Make me barf!" Courtney yelled.

We were all cracking up.

"You know, we were very, very lucky," Mom

said. "There have been no cases of anyone actually eating any of the potatoes."

"Can you imagine if someone had?" Max said.

Dad walked back into the room, holding an open can of dog food. "What do you suppose would have happened?" he asked.

"I don't even want to think about it," Mom said.

"Yappy!" Dad called out. "Oh, Yappy! Has anyone seen him?"

Max rolled his eyes. "He's been in hiding since the trouble started. Some brave pup."

Dad nodded. "That means the walk-in closet. He loves the smell of shoes."

I ran into Mom and Dad's room. The walk-in closet door was closed. I pushed on it, but it wouldn't budge.

"Yappy?" I called out.

I heard a loud thump. The door started to crack, as if something were pushing against it, from inside.

Something huge.

GRRRRRRRRRRRRRRR ...

Slowly I backed away. My arm hairs were standing on end.

"*Yappy?*"

About the Author

Peter Lerangis is also the author of *It Came from the Cafeteria* and the popular Hopnoodle books: *Spring Fever!* and its sequel, *Spring Break*. He lives in New York City with his wife, Tina deVaron, and their two sons, Nicholas and Joseph. Mr. Lerangis has never actually met a killer potato, but he recently encountered some elephant garlic. He is considering a book about it. But don't hold your breath.

GOT
Goosebumps
YET?
by R.L. Stine

--------- GOOSEBUMPS ---------

--------- GOOSEBUMPS PRESENTS ---------

❏ BAB93954-8	TV Episode #7: My Hairiest Adventure	$3.99
❏ BAB93955-6	TV Episode #8: Be Careful What You Wish For	$3.99
❏ BAB93959-9	TV Episode #9: Go Eat Worms!	$3.99
❏ BAB62836-4	Tales to Give You Goosebumps Book & Light Set Special Edition #1	$11.95
❏ BAB26603-9	More Tales to Give You Goosebumps Book & Light Set Special Edition #2	$11.95
❏ BAB74150-4	Even More Tales to Give You Goosebumps Book and Boxer Shorts Pack Special Edition #3	$14.99

──────── GIVE YOURSELF GOOSEBUMPS ────────

❏ BAB55323-2	#1: Escape from the Carnival of Horrors	$3.99
❏ BAB56645-8	#2: Tick Tock, You're Dead	$3.99
❏ BAB56646-6	#3: Trapped in Bat Wing Hall	$3.99
❏ BAB67318-1	#4: The Deadly Experiments of Dr. Eeek	$3.99
❏ BAB67319-X	#5: Night in Werewolf Woods	$3.99
❏ BAB67320-3	#6: Beware of the Purple Peanut Butter	$3.99
❏ BAB67321-1	#7: Under the Magician's Spell	$3.99
❏ BAB84765-1	#8: The Curse of the Creeping Coffin	$3.99
❏ BAB84766-X	#9: The Knight in Screaming Armor	$3.99
❏ BAB84767-8	#10: Diary of a Mad Mummy	$3.99
❏ BAB84768-6	#11: Deep in the Jungle of Doom	$3.99
❏ BAB84772-4	#12: Welcome to the Wicked Wax Museum	$3.99
❏ BAB84773-2	#13: Scream of the Evil Genie	$3.99
❏ BAB84774-0	#14: The Creepy Creations of Professor Shock	$3.99

❏ BAB53770-9	The Goosebumps Monster Blood Pack	$11.95
❏ BAB50995-0	The Goosebumps Monster Edition #1	$12.95
❏ BAB93371-X	The Goosebumps Monster Edition #2	$12.95
❏ BAB60265-9	Goosebumps Official Collector's Caps Collecting Kit	$5.99
❏ BAB73906-9	Goosebumps Postcard Book	$7.95
❏ BAB73902-6	The 1997 Goosebumps 365 Scare-a-Day Calendar	$8.95
❏ BAB73907-7	The Goosebumps 1997 Wall Calendar	$10.99

Scare me, thrill me, mail me GOOSEBUMPS now!

Available wherever you buy books, or use this order form. Scholastic Inc., P.O. Box 7502,
2931 East McCarty Street, Jefferson City, MO 65102

Please send me the books I have checked above. I am enclosing $_____ (please add $2.00 to cover shipping and handling). Send check or money order — no cash or C.O.D.s please.

Name _____ Age _____

Address _____

City _____ State/Zip _____

Please allow four to six weeks for delivery. Offer good in the U.S. only. Sorry, mail orders are not available to residents of Canada. Prices subject to change.

GB796

ALIENS, GHOSTS, AND MONSTERS!

The scariest creatures you'd ever want to meet in nine terrifying collections from Bruce Coville that will make you shake, shiver...and scream!

- ☐ BAV46162-1 Bruce Coville's Book of Aliens:
  Tales to Warp Your Mind.................................$3.99
- ☐ BAV85293-0 Bruce Coville's Book of Aliens II........................$3.99
- ☐ BAV46160-5 Bruce Coville's Book of Ghosts:
  Tales to Haunt You..$3.99
- ☐ BAV85294-9 Bruce Coville's Book of Ghosts II:
  More Tales to Haunt You...............................$3.99
- ☐ BAV25931-8 Bruce Coville's Book of Magic:
  Tales to Cast a Spell on You.........................$3.99
- ☐ BAV46159-1 Bruce Coville's Book of Monsters:
  Tales to Give You the Creeps.......................$3.99
- ☐ BAV85292-2 Bruce Coville's Book of Monsters II
  More Tales to Give You the Creeps.............$3.99
- ☐ BAV46161-3 Bruce Coville's Book of Nightmares:
  Tales to Make You Scream............................$3.99
- ☐ BAV25930-X Bruce Coville's Book of Spine Tinglers:
  Tales to Make You Shiver.............................$3.99

A GLC BOOK

Available wherever you buy books, or use this order form.

Scholastic Inc., P.O. Box 7502, 2931 East McCarty Street, Jefferson City, MO 65102

Please send me the books I have checked above. I am enclosing $_____
(please add $2.00 to cover shipping and handling.) Send check or money order
— no cash or C.O.D.s please.

Name_____Birthdate_____

Address _____

City _____State/Zip_____

Please allow four to six weeks for delivery. Offer good in the U.S.A. only. Sorry, mail orders are not available
to residents of Canada. Prices subject to change.

BC696

APPLE® PAPERBACKS

Pick an Apple and Polish Off Some Great Reading!

BEST-SELLING APPLE TITLES

❑ MT43944-8	**Afternoon of the Elves** Janet Taylor Lisle	**$2.99**
❑ MT41624-3	**The Captive** Joyce Hansen	**$3.50**
❑ MT43266-4	**Circle of Gold** Candy Dawson Boyd	**$3.50**
❑ MT44064-0	**Class President** Johanna Hurwitz	**$3.50**
❑ MT45436-6	**Cousins** Virginia Hamilton	**$3.50**
❑ MT43130-7	**The Forgotten Door** Alexander Key	**$2.95**
❑ MT44569-3	**Freedom Crossing** Margaret Goff Clark	**$3.50**
❑ MT42858-6	**Hot and Cold Summer** Johanna Hurwitz	**$3.50**
❑ MT25514-2	**The House on Cherry Street 2: The Horror** Rodman Philbrick and Lynn Harnett	**$3.50**
❑ MT41708-8	**The Secret of NIMH** Robert C. O'Brien	**$3.99**
❑ MT42882-9	**Sixth Grade Sleepover** Eve Bunting	**$3.50**
❑ MT42537-4	**Snow Treasure** Marie McSwigan	**$3.50**
❑ MT42378-9	**Thank You, Jackie Robinson** Barbara Cohen	**$3.99**